P9-CLH-228

E CZERNECKI
Czernecki, Stefan, 1946-
Lilliput 5357 /

**PALM BEACH COUNTY
LIBRARY SYSTEM**
3650 Summit Boulevard
West Palm Beach, FL 33406-4198

ZOOM

ZOOM

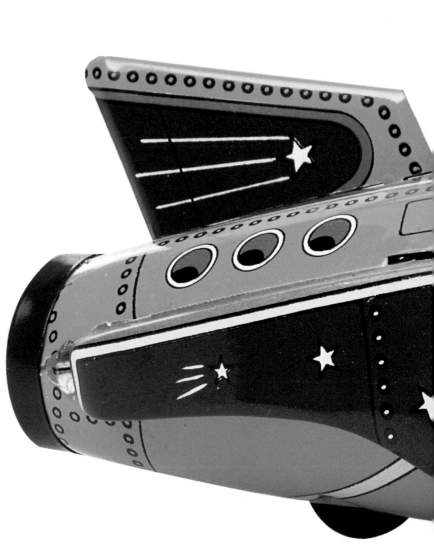

To the memory of Hideaki Honda, a valued friend, professor of Children's Literature, Sagami Women's University, Tokyo

And for Eriya Tamura, Tokyo

First published in 2006 by Simply Read Books
www.simplyreadbooks.com

Copyright © 2006 by Stefan Czernecki
All rights reserved. No part of this publication may be reproduced, stored in a retrieval system or transmitted, in any form or by any means, without the written permission of the publisher.

Cataloguing in Publication Data

Czernecki, Stefan, 1946–
  Lilliput 5357 / written and illustrated by Stefan Czernecki / 1st edition

ISBN 1-894965-32-9

  1. Picture books for children. I. Title

PS8555.Z49L54 2005   jC813'.54   C2005-903294-4

The toys and robots used to create the illustrations for this book are used by permission of Schylling Associates, Inc.; Rocket USA, Inc.; Blaze Metal Space Art; and A Bakers Dozen Antiques.

While every effort has been made to obtain permission to use material, there may be cases where we have been unable to trace the creator. The publisher will be happy to correct any obmissions in future printings.

Many thanks to the following people for their help in the preparation of this book: Heather Baker, Pauline Lawson, Tiffany Stone, Ricki Ewings, Terry Clark, Yukiko Tosa, Mary Eaglesham, Douglas McCaffry, Cesar Vargas, Keri MacRae, Sohta Takashima, Dylan Schofield, Howard Ursuliak.

Color separations by Scanlab - Canada

Printed in China

10 9 8 7 6 5 4 3 2 1

Book design by Katsumi Hirotani - Japan
Photography by Lincoln Heller - USA
Digital imaging by Miles Harrison - Canada

Lilliput 5357

Stefan Czernecki

Simply Read Books

Tick-Tock

Tick-Tock

Ring-a-Ding-Ding

Every morning Lilliput 5357 wound up his motor
and marched out to play.

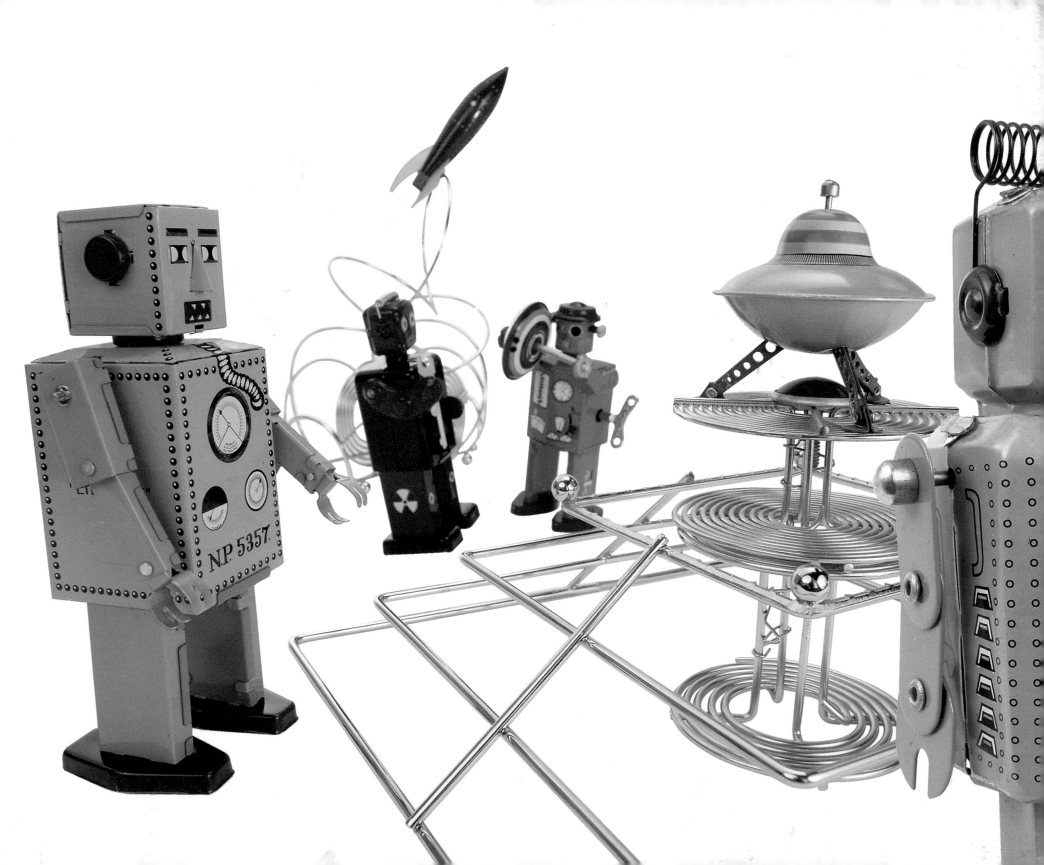

But then one morning...

BIG robots with BAD attitudes showed up.

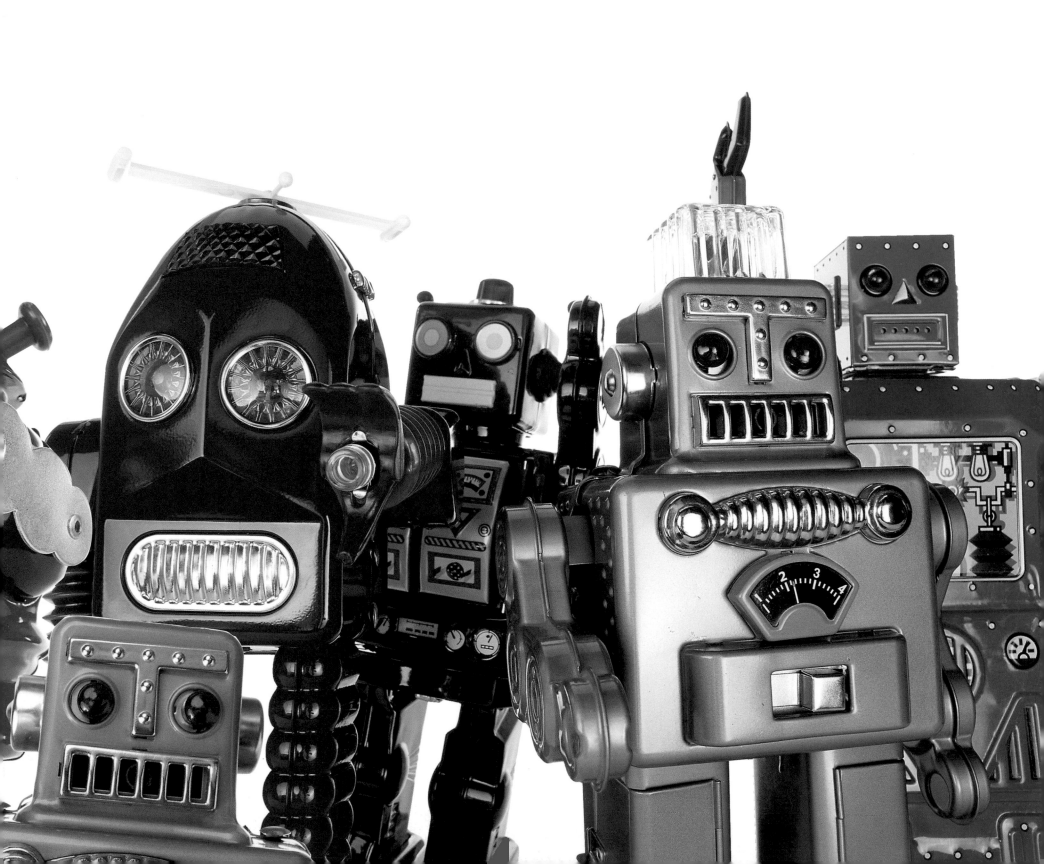

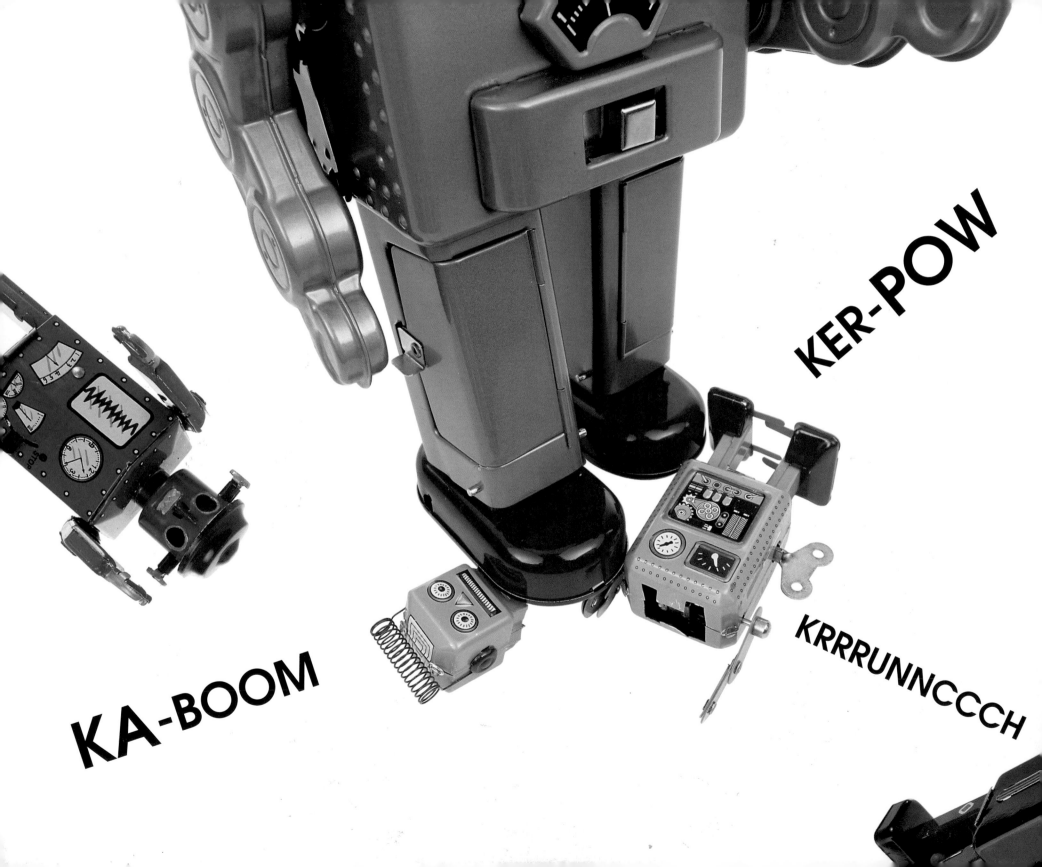

KER-POW

KA-BOOM

KRRRUNNCCCH

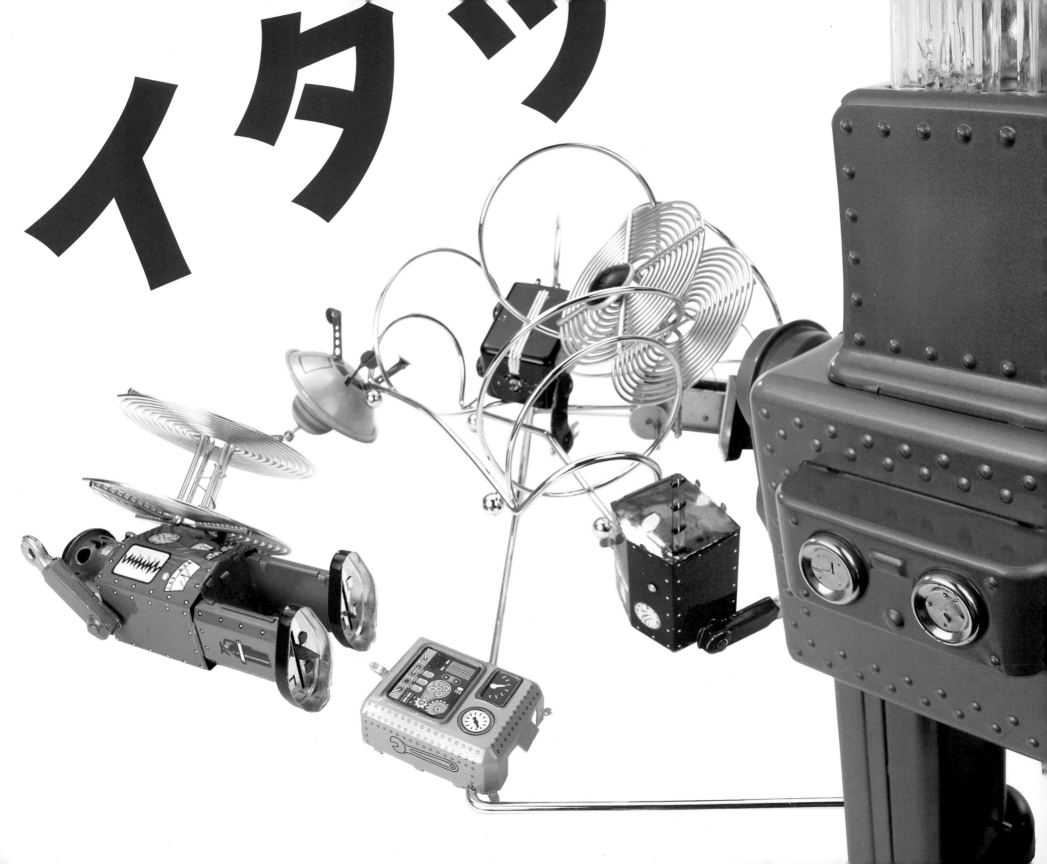

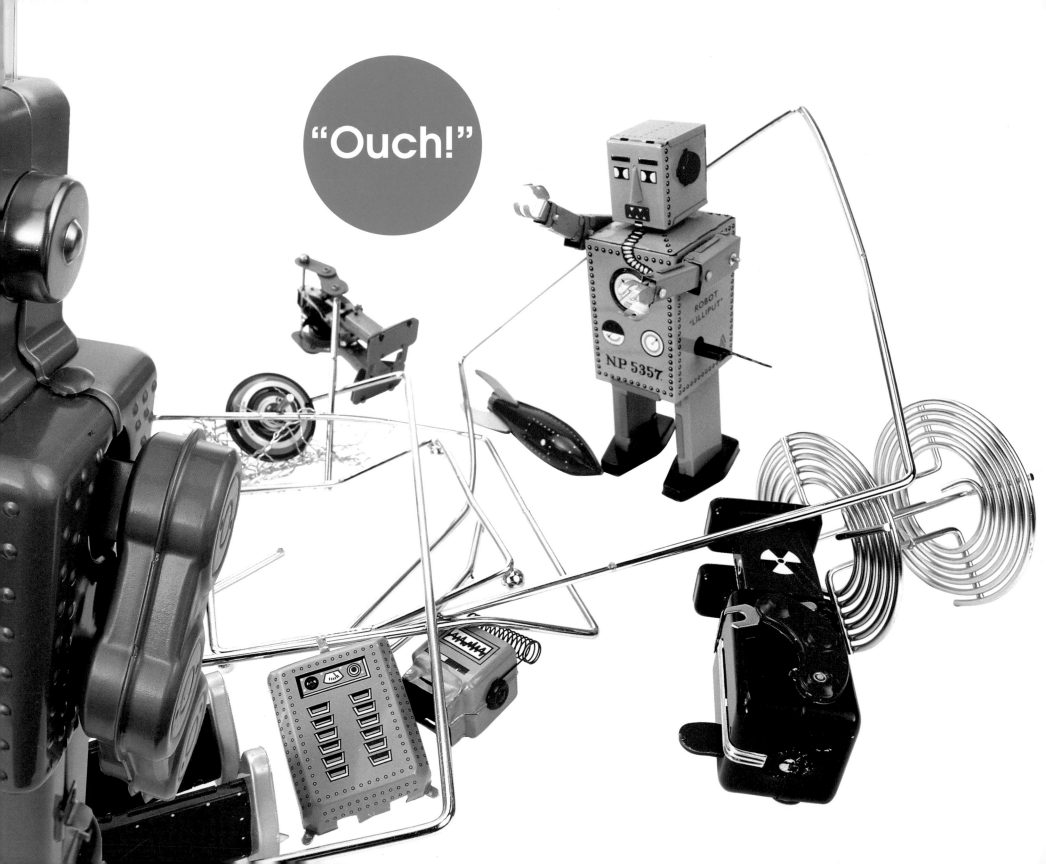

"Where am I going to play NOW?"

Lilliput checked his DIRECTIONAL DIMENSIONAL DECODER and headed off.

The first place he came to was a CROSSWALK.

VROOM VROOM

HONK **HONK**

CLANK CLANK

"YIKES! TOO NOISY!"

Lilliput drove on.

The second place he came to
was a GARBAGE DUMP.

EEUUWW

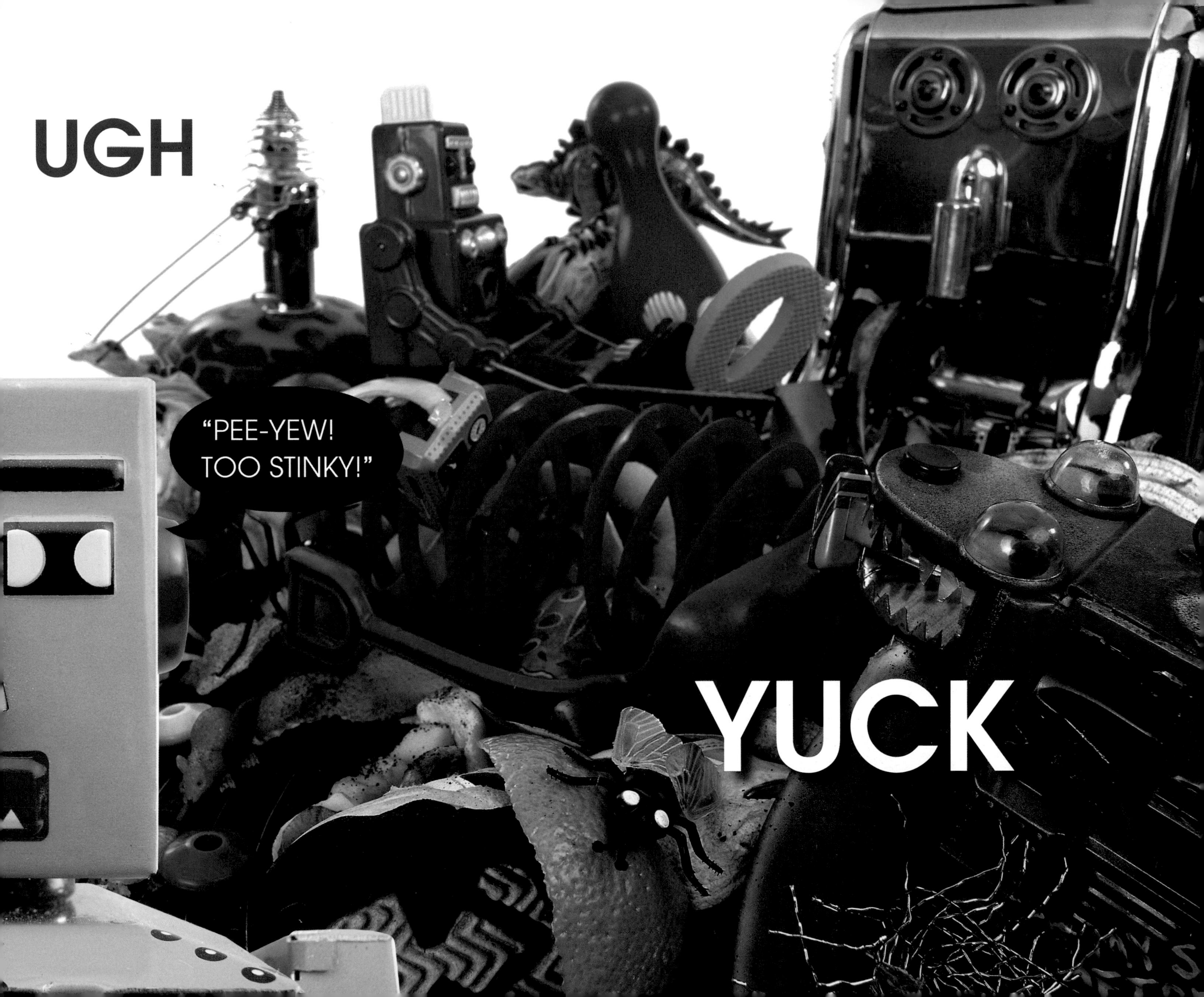
UGH
"PEE-YEW! TOO STINKY!"
YUCK

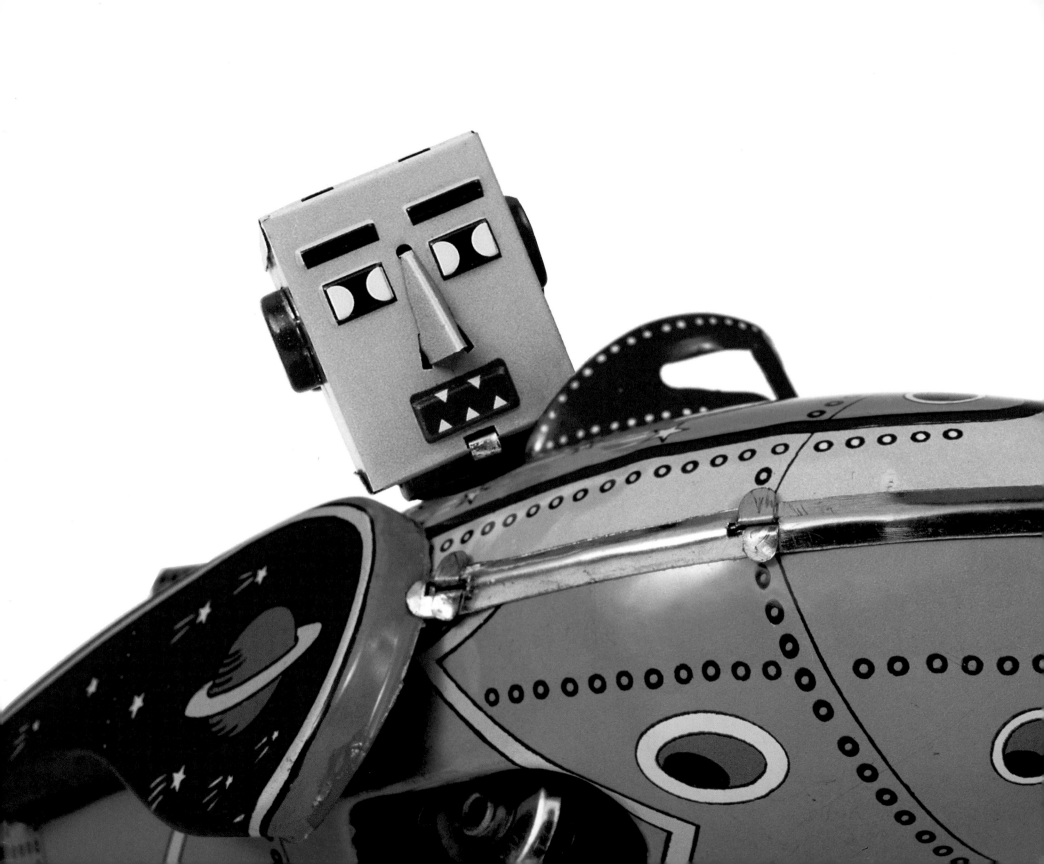

Lilliput stepped hard on the pedal and raced away.

ピ

SQUEEEEEAL

SCREEEEEECH

Lilliput hit the HYPERDRIVE BUTTON.

Suddenly he was somewhere

ICKY, STICKY, OOEEY

"Will I EVER find a new place to play?"

and GOOEY.

BLEEP BLEEP BLEEP

A FLYING SAUCER appeared above him.

Out stepped friendly ASTRO GUYS
from a distant galaxy.
"Hello 5357. Are you lost?"

Lilliput told his sad story.

リリプット
5357

"We know a place you will like."

In a flash

Lilliput was beamed across

INTERSTELLAR SPACE

to a playground on a planet

inhabited by friendly ROBOTEERS.

BIPPITY ZIPPITY BEEP BEEP BEEP

Soon Lilliput was having fun...